"I was born in London in 1946 and grew up in a sweet shop in Essex. For several years I worked as a graphic designer, but in 1980 I decided to concentrate on writing and illustrating books for children.

My wife, Annette, and I have two grown-up children, Ben and Amanda, and we have put down roots in Suffolk.

I haven't recently counted how many books there are with my name on the cover but Percy the Park Keeper accounts for a good many of them. I'm reliably informed that they have sold more than three million copies. Hooray!

I didn't realise this when I invented Percy, but I can now see that he's very like my mum's dad, my grandpa. I even have a picture of him giving a ride to my brother and me in his old home-made wooden wheelbarrow!"

NICK BUTTERWORTH

PERCY'S FRIEND
THE FOX

NICK BUTTERWORTH

Collins

An imprint of HarperCollinsPublishers

Thanks Graham Daldry. You're a wizard.

Thanks Atholl McDonald. You're a hero!

First published in Great Britain by HarperCollins Publishers Ltd in 2001

1 3 5 7 9 10 8 6 4 2

ISBN: 0 00 711977 1

Text and illustrations copyright © Nick Butterworth 2001
The author asserts the moral right to be identified as the author of the work.

A CIP catalogue record for this title is available from the British Library.
The HarperCollins website address is: www.**fire**and**water**.com

Printed and bound in Belgium

MY FRIEND
THE FOX

Some foxes can be sneaky,
but not this one. He's very
friendly and he's funny too, usually when
he doesn't mean to be!

He says he can read but I do wonder
about that because he often holds the book
upside down. Then he'll start reading in a
peculiar, low voice. "Grrworr ffss hhee-hhee
grrrwll pipipip ffss grrhoo..."

He says it's a special way of speaking that
only foxes understand.

Once, when he came to stay for the
night in my hut, he said he
thought his feet were
sticking out of bed, so he
got out to have a look.

"It's alright," he said.
"They weren't."

Some of my friends may not agree with me, but I really think the fox is very musical. I don't know anyone else who could play Jingle Bells on the icicles.

I know a bit about music (I play the accordion) and I think it must be very hard to play anything at all on the icicles, especially when some of your best notes keep breaking off.

THE FOX REALLY LIKES . . .

Giving presents. I'm afraid he's not very
good at wrapping them, but he tries hard.

Climbing. He's particularly good at *Up*.
He is not quite so good at *Down*.

THE FOX DOESN'T LIKE ...

Hide-and-seek. For some strange reason, he always seems to be the first to be found.

Shadows. Not if they're not his own.
Not at night, anyway.

Just once or twice, the fox has come knocking on my door because he has had a bad dream. But this one wasn't a bad dream at all. He told me he'd had a dream about a picnic tree.

He must have gone to bed feeling hungry!
He said that there were all sorts of things
to eat hanging from the branches.
   Even the spaces between some of the
branches made the shapes of picnic food,
                 but that wasn't so good
                      because you can't
                            eat spaces.

I've got lots of pictures in my photo album.

When the fox came to a fancy dress party, he wore a fancy dress!

The fox always enjoys a game of conkers.

The sky at night is very strange.
It's close and far away.
It just goes on for ever and ever
And ever and ever and ever and ever and ever and ever and ever and ever and ever and ever

FAVOURITE PLACES

One of the fox's favourite places is one of
mine, too. On a sunny afternoon he likes
nothing better than to snooze lazily in a
hammock.

I put this hammock up for myself, but I
had to leave it to sort out a little problem for
the mice. When I came back, there was the
fox! He said that he had found the hammock
empty, and as nobody seemed to want it, it
was a shame to waste it.

When he's feeling more energetic, you will sometimes find the fox playing by the bandstand. There's a statue of a horse nearby. When he thinks nobody is looking, the fox will jump on the horse's back and pretend to go for a ride.

Perhaps the fox's favourite place of all is his home in the tree house. It's one of my favourite places, too, because I know that's where I'll find my friend the fox!

Here he is, outside his own front door. The fox is full of fun, usually smiling and he's always pleased to see you.

THE TREE HOUSE

In this picture you'll see Percy the Park Keeper and his friends. But if you look very carefully, you can also find a balloon, a kite, a hot-water bottle, a model aeroplane, a paintbrush, a robin, a beach ball, a magpie, a go-go, Percy's stripy mug, a pencil, a conker, Percy's watering can, a cheese roll, a framed picture of Percy, one of Percy's gardening gloves, a model yacht, a plastic duck, a banana, and a frog. Oh, and ten ladybirds!

FREE GIANT POSTER

Nick Butterworth's new, giant picture of the tree house
in Percy's Park shows Percy and all his animal friends
in and around their tree house home. There are also
lots of things hidden in the picture. Some are easy
to find. Some are much harder!

To send off for your free poster, simply snip off
FOUR tokens, each from a different book in the
Percy the Park Keeper and his Friends series and send them
to the address below. Remember to include
your name, address and age.

Percy Poster, Children's Marketing Department,
Harper Collins Publishers, 77-85 Fulham Palace Road, London W6 8JB

Offer applies to UK and Eire only. Available while stocks last.
Allow 28 days for delivery.

Read all the stories about Percy and his animal friends...

THE OWL'S LESSON — NICK BUTTERWORTH

OWL TAKES CHARGE — NICK BUTTERWORTH

THE BADGER'S BATH — NICK BUTTERWORTH

THE LOST ACORNS — NICK BUTTERWORTH

ONE WARM FOX — NICK BUTTERWORTH

THE FOX'S HICCUPS — NICK BUTTERWORTH

THE HEDGEHOG'S BALLOON — NICK BUTTERWORTH

THE CROSS RABBIT — NICK BUTTERWORTH

AFTER THE STORM — NICK BUTTERWORTH

ONE SNOWY NIGHT — NICK BUTTERWORTH

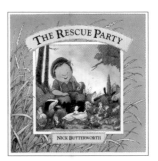

THE RESCUE PARTY — NICK BUTTERWORTH

THE TREASURE HUNT — NICK BUTTERWORTH

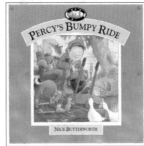

PERCY'S BUMPY RIDE — NICK BUTTERWORTH

THE SECRET PATH — NICK BUTTERWORTH

Percy the Park Keeper Games Book

A Year with Percy Colouring Book — NICK BUTTERWORTH

Percy the Park Keeper 1·2·3 — NICK BUTTERWORTH

Percy the Park Keeper A·B·C — NICK BUTTERWORTH

Percy toys and videos
are also available.